Unspeakable

Written and Illustrated by

James D. Lopez

Unspeakable

Text, illustrations, and concept © 2016, by James D. Lopez

ALL RIGHTS RESERVED

No part of this book may be used or reproduced in any manner whatever without the prior written permission of both the publisher and the copyright owner.

ISBN-13: 978-0-692-61959-9
ISBN-10: 0-692-61959-3
Library of Congress Control Number: 2016902460
Little Gnome Publications/James D. Lopez: Los Angeles, CA

First Edition

It would take the length of an entire novel to list each and every person who made this work possible. I offer a simple thank-you to all my loved ones—you know who you are.

Also, an especially big thank-you goes to my beautiful Tonya: I love you, always and forever.

Trigger Warning:

There is none.

1

Annie was washing her face before going to bed that night. After patting her face dry, she glanced in the bathroom mirror at her own reflection. "My complexion is finally clearing up," she thought to herself. And then her reflection winked at her.

Or so she thought.

"I must be tired," she said aloud. She walked over to her bedroom, collapsed onto her bed, and fell asleep.

***

Annie washed her face before going to bed, which was her usual routine. When she had finished drying her face, she looked into the mirror at her own reflection. She stared at her own image for a moment or two.

And then her reflection winked at her.

He walked into his bedroom and over to his closet. He grabbed the knob and stepped in, looking for his suit jacket. It was a walk-in closet. As he felt between the various shirts and other items, he caught a glimpse of something shiny. He took a closer look. It was a knife. And she was holding it.

Phineas loved dressing and performing as a birthday clown. It ensured him an audience, and it allowed him to interact with the local children. After several hours of telling jokes and folding up balloon animals at Amber's fifth birthday party, he caught a glimpse of two-year-old Lucy smiling at him. He smiled back, noting to himself how much she resembled her sister, Amber. After Amber finished opening up her presents and the cake was cut and distributed, the children ran off into the yard to play while the grown-ups gathered around in the living room to have a few drinks and chat with one another. Things went on this way until Donna Cortez, the birthday girl's mother, received a call on her phone. As she answered, she realized that it was from the company she had contacted to hire the clown for Amber's party.

"I'm very sorry," the manager stated, "but Zippo the clown was unable to make it today due to a car accident."

Donna was puzzled. "What are you talking about?" she asked the manager. "Phineas the clown has been with us for the past several hours."

There was an awkward pause. "We don't have anyone in our company who goes by the name of Phineas, Ms. Cortez," the manager stated. "Zippo was our only available employee, and he couldn't make it today."

Donna put the phone down immediately and rushed out into the yard to find Phineas.

He was nowhere to be found.

And Lucy was missing.

Karl headed home as quickly as he could. He knew that his wife, Linda, was especially agitated today, and the fact that he had to work late didn't make things any better. He loved her and was prepared to deal with her episodes for the rest of his life. Still, in his own mind, it didn't help that she would stop taking her medication every now and then. This led to several incidents in the past that cost her some jobs of her own. He tried to call her before he took off, but there was no response. When he finally made it to his apartment door, he tried to open it, but the door seemed stuck. He tried dialing his wife on the phone, but there was no response. "Linda," he called aloud, hoping that she would hear him through the door.

Still, there was no reply.

Karl resorted to attempting to budge his way into the door. After what felt like several hours, he managed to clear about a three-inch space. Feeling confident, he continued to force his way into his front room. It wasn't locked by any means, but something was preventing him from getting it open all the way. Continuing to labor, he managed to make an opening large enough for him to squeeze through. He pushed a leg in first, followed by a shoulder and, eventually, his head. As he glanced over, he saw what was blocking the door: it was his wife's lifeless body. Lying a few feet away from her body was an empty bottle of pills.

Alice had just shot an intruder in the dark. It was in the middle of the night when she woke up to the sound of broken glass. She managed to grab the handgun from the closet before investigating the sound. It was very dark in the house. As she made her way to the living room, she saw a large human figure make its way into the room through the broken window. "Stop!" said Alice upon catching a glimpse of the intruder. "Get out right now or I'll shoot!" The figure paid no attention and started toward her in a clumsy, awkward gait. She pulled the trigger and shot at the intruder three times. The body fell with a thud. Alice made her way over to the nearest source of light and turned it on. There was no blood on the floor, but she could make out some bullet holes in the figure's chest. As she looked at the large body, she saw it for what it was—a ragdoll.

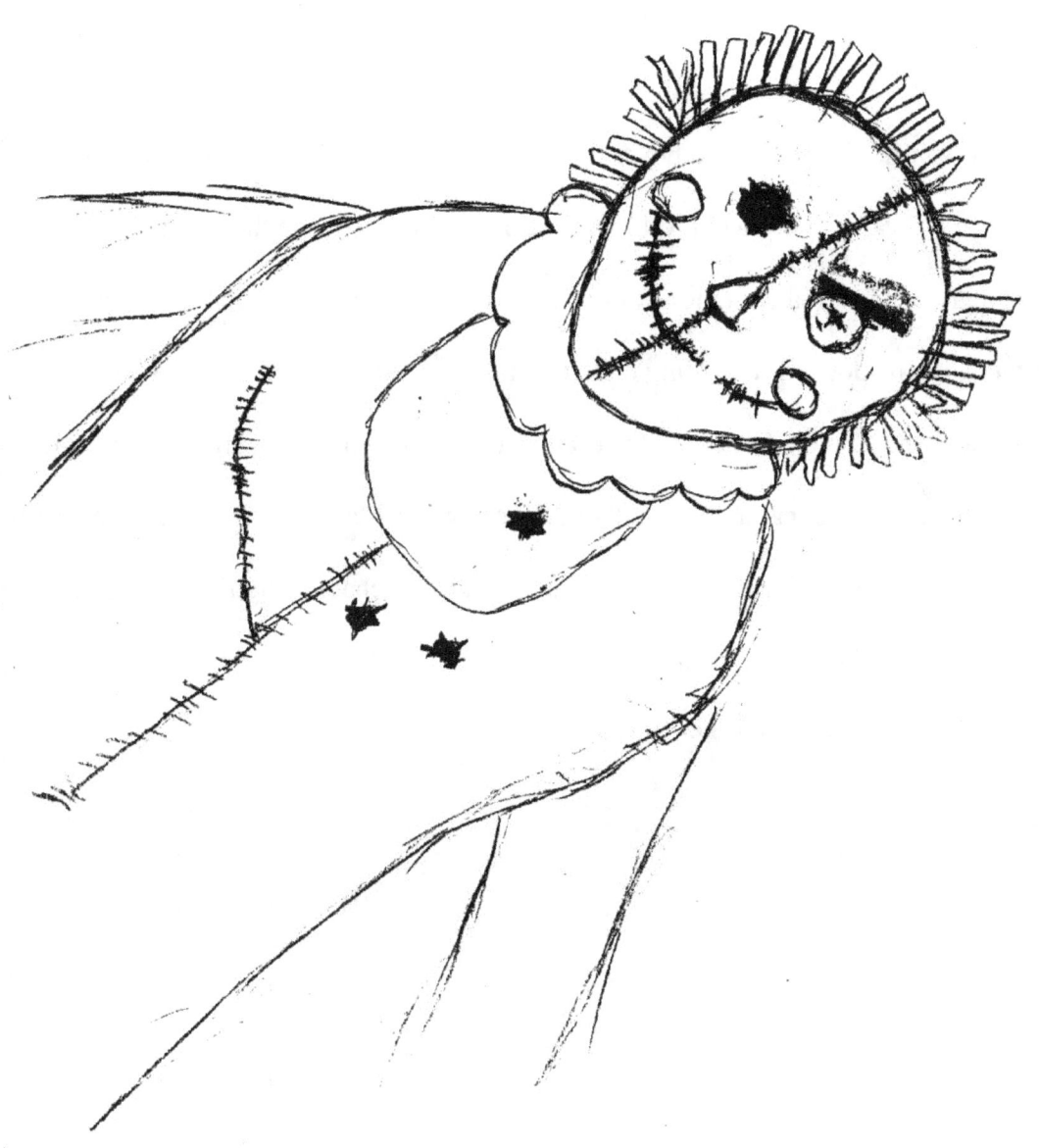

Sixteen-year-old Michael was enjoying having the whole house to himself. His parents were out of town for the weekend. Being a bit of an introvert, he opted to spend his Saturday night staying up late watching movies. As the night progressed, he decided to turn off all the lights in the house, as he preferred the feeling of spending a quiet evening in the dark. Besides, the TV provided more than enough light for his liking. About halfway into the latest movie, he looked over from the couch at his left side and noticed what appeared to be a patch of soft light. It was close to the wall, which was several feet away from him, and yet it wasn't exactly touching the wall; instead, it appeared to hover in midair. In terms of shape, rather than coming in the form of a ray, it was more of a dull orb. "I must be getting tired," he thought to himself. He turned his attention back to the movie. A few minutes later, Michael glanced at his left. The orb was still there, but he noticed something different this time, although he couldn't quite pinpoint what exactly he saw. Then slowly, the orb began to move in his direction. As it came closer and closer, he could see that in the middle of the orb was a human arm. The arm appeared to be wrapped, or rather, clothed, in the sleeve of a suit jacket. Michael couldn't see whom, or what, the arm was attached to; it just seemed suspended in space. The index finger pointed straight at him as the arm came closer and closer.

Bertha rushed into the bedroom of her five-year-old daughter, Elizabeth. It was close to 3:00 a.m. in the morning, and the sound of Elizabeth's screams woke her up. As Bertha hugged and comforted her daughter, she asked her, "What happened?"

"Mommy! He's here!" the little girl replied frantically. "He's here! I saw him under my bed!"

As was usually the case when Elizabeth had a nightmare, Bertha turned the main light on in the room and had Elizabeth check with her for monsters under the bed. They then looked in the closet as well as any spot in the room that a monster would be able to hide in. "There's nothing here, baby," said Bertha as she kissed her daughter and began to tuck her in. "You be my big, brave girl, ok?"

"Yes, Mommy," said Elizabeth. "Good night."

Bertha turned the main light off, returned to her own bedroom, and got into bed.

Even though she trusted her mother, Elizabeth decided to take one last look over the side of her bed to be sure that no monsters were hiding underneath. As she did this, two things slowly slid into her view: a hand and a hoof.

There was a large black box sitting in the middle of the living room. Manny had never seen it before. He went to his parents' bedroom to ask them about it. While they were both extremely annoyed with him for waking them up after midnight, they reported that they were unaware of any black, wooden boxes being brought into their apartment. They then fell back asleep.

Manny was puzzled, as he certainly hadn't brought it into their home himself, and the three of them were the only ones there that day. He went back into the living room to investigate, but the box had disappeared. Although he was still intrigued and confused by what seemed to have taken place, he decided to go back to his bedroom and try to get some more sleep. As soon as he got in there, he heard the sound of something being dragged across the living room floor. He returned to the living room and saw the black box again. More curious than ever, he decided to take a peek at what was inside the box. As he opened it, he was disappointed to find it completely empty. He closed the box and looked up across the hallway to his bedroom door, which was open halfway. Something appeared to be slowly coming out of hiding from behind the door, and Manny caught a glimpse of a grinning, mask-like face peering at him.

After grabbing ahold of his victim, the aggressor immediately began to slap her repeatedly using the back of his hand. To his knowledge, there was no one else in the parking lot. She struggled to break away from him, but he held onto her and continued to beat her without stopping.

***

His slaps turned into punches as he continued to beat his victim down. When she was on the ground, he crouched on top of her and continued to hit her, even though she was bleeding and barely conscious.

***

The aggressor pulled out a sharp knife from his back pocket and slit his victim's throat.

***

He then punctured his victim a few times in the chest and abdomen, even though she was already dead.

***

He planted a kiss on his victim's cheek, followed by a kiss on her lips. He then got up and ran away.

***

From the safety of the bushes that enclosed the parking lot, an observer looked around to make sure that the aggressor, or rather, the murderer, had truly vacated the lot. It approached the body of the woman and proceeded to caress her dead face. The observer then touched its own face, moving its fingers over the permanently painted grin etched onto a head made of porcelain.

Calvin had just finished parking. He opened the trunk of his car and lifted up a relatively large bundle from it. He slung it over his shoulder, opened the front door to his house, and carried it inside. As he locked the front door, he smiled to himself as he thought of just how pleased his mother would be. He made his way to the very back of the house and knocked on the door to his mother's bedroom. "Mom!" he called out through the door. "I brought you your dinner!" At first, there was nothing but silence. Then, he heard the sound of a chain being unfastened, and the door opened up a few inches. Calvin bent down and placed the bundle on the floor; he then began to unwrap it. Calvin's mother drooled in anticipation as she saw what her son had brought for her: it was a child, no more than five years old. She then dragged the lifeless body into her room and shut the door behind her.

I think of all the things I have to do

as I make my way onto the train.

I am on my way home.

    I can see you from a safe distance.

    I watch you come and go every day.

    You're beautiful.

It's another day at work.

Another day, another dollar.

    I can see you.

    I'm always watching you.

    God, you're beautiful.

I am on my way home.

    I watch you come and go every day.

Another day and I am on my way home.

    I watch you come and go every day.

I have been watching you for a long time.

    I want to know you.

    I want to be with you.

    You're so beautiful.

I get on the train to go home.

    I am with you on the train.

The journey feels a bit longer than usual.

I want to see where you live.

I am off now.

I am walking; just a few more minutes

and I'll be home.

I am with you.

I want to see you.

Who's there?

(Silence)

I thought I saw…

Never mind.

(Silence)

I make my way into my room.

I can see you.

I am with you.

Who's there?

(Silence)

WHO'S THERE!?!?

(I make my presence known).

…

...

She's gone!

SHE'S GONE!!!!

    (sob)

    I hold her body in my hands…

    I just wanted to love you…

    Why couldn't you say yes?

    WHY COULDN'T YOU SAY YES?!?!

The wind blew as the crowd cheered at the gathering. It was a light wind, but enough to sway a body—more specifically, the body that hung at the gallows. Executions continued to be a crowd pleaser. A crowd pleaser: that is exactly how the hangman looked at himself. He smiled as he admired his handiwork, taking in the applause and cheers coming from the crowd of spectators. He loved his job all right, and there was never any shortage of people awaiting his justice.

"We need to talk."

Jeremy was always nervous about seeing his doctor, even though he had always been in relatively good physical health; however, he found Dr. Chong's request to talk especially unnerving.

"We now have the results of the x-rays on that lump at the small of your back," said the doctor. Her voice was calm, but she had a very serious look on her face. "How long has it been there?"

"Well," began Jeremy, trying to gather himself, "it started off as something the size of a pimple, but that was two months ago. It is now the size of a mango." Dr. Chong paused for a second; she then said, "I at first thought that it was a tumor, but…wait a minute. Let me try something." She then took out her stethoscope and placed it on top of the lump. "I might as well cut to the chase. The x-rays showed a fully developed human skeleton inside the lump. But there's one more thing: I can also detect a steady heartbeat."

Mayra had a little poodle named Trinket. Mayra adored Trinket; her husband, Tim, on the other hand, did not like the dog. Trinket had constantly barked and nipped at him since the very beginning. Mayra coddled the dog and enabled all his actions, even if they were aggressive or annoying. "What harm can a little thing like this do?" she asked whenever friends, neighbors, and relatives told her that she needed to discipline him. Tim had smacked him once, only for Trinket to run to the safety of Mayra's arms; while he did this, he continued to bark and snarl at Tim.

As it happened one night, Tim got home from work and found himself alone—well, almost alone; Trinket, of course, was there to keep him company, barking and yapping the whole time. Tim knew that Mayra would be out visiting relatives in the evening, so he wasn't surprised. Still, the dog was a handful no matter what the circumstances happened to be. As he made his way over to the fridge for a beer, he felt a tug at the hem of his pants; it was Trinket, of course, snarling the whole time. Then an idea occurred to Tim. He decided to do something he had wanted to do for a long time, and with Mayra gone, it felt like the perfect moment. He made his way over to his closet (with Trinket still biting on the hem of his pants) and found exactly what he was looking for. It had been a long time since he had last seen or used it, but an appropriate moment had finally presented itself. Tim looked at Trinket and smiled at him for the first time as he produced the object he was looking for: his old hunting pistol, fully loaded.

Infinitum